THE TALE OF
TUTANKHAMUN'S
TREASURE

ReadZone Books Limited

www.ReadZoneBooks.com

© in this edition 2016 ReadZone Books Limited

This print edition published in cooperation with Fiction Express, who first published this title in weekly instalments as an interactive e-book.

FICTION EXPRESS

Fiction Express
Boolino Limited
First Floor Office, 2 College Street,
Ludlow, Shropshire SY8 1AN
www.fictionexpress.co.uk

Find out more about Fiction Express on pages 114–115.

Design: Laura Harrison & Keith Williams
Cover Image: Bigstock

© in the text 2016 Alex Woolf
The moral right of the author has been asserted.

ISBN 978-1-78322-601-6

Printed in Malta by Melita Press

THE TIME DETECTIVES

THE TALE OF TUTANKHAMUN'S TREASURE

ALEX WOOLF

FICTION EXPRESS

What do other readers think?

Here are some comments left on the Fiction Express blog about this book:

"Hello we're really enjoying the book so far and it's cool to imagine the scene of two adventurers exploring Ancient Egypt. Thanks for making this amazing book."
Max and Rob, Telford

"[We] rate the book a 10 out of 10, it is really cool because travelling back in time is really fun."
Zander, Owen and Casey, Ludlow Junior School

"I love this book so far it is so imaginative and I hope theres a sequel."
Archie, Chelmsford, Essex

"The best book I've ever read"
"I like the story because it was adventurous and exciting."
"Amazing and surprising!"
**Pupils from Wrekin Class,
Worfield Endowed CE School**

Contents

Chapter 1	A Letter from a King	7
Chapter 2	A Necklace	19
Chapter 3	Saving a Life	27
Chapter 4	A Suspect	38
Chapter 5	A Dangerous Rivalry	48
Chapter 6	Accusations	61
Chapter 7	A Deadly Poison	69
Chapter 8	Last Chances	78
Chapter 9	Execution Day	90
Chapter 10	The Evidence	102
About Fiction Express		114
About the Author		120

Cast of Main Characters

Here is a list of the main characters that appear in this book:

Joe and Maya, time-travelling detectives

King Tutankhamun, the Pharaoh of Egypt

Queen Ankhe, wife of Tutankhamun

Lord Ay, Grand Vizier, one of Tutankhamun's trusted advisors

Tey, wife of Lord Ay

Mahu, Chief of Police

Horem, General of the Armies, another trusted advisor to Tutankhamun

Bek, a young priest accused of theft

To my cats, Juno and Minerva,
who would have loved ancient Egypt.

Chapter 1

A Letter from a King

The lights dimmed. The audience ceased their murmuring. On the stage, beneath a single spotlight, stood a small, silver-haired Egyptian woman. She placed a gloved hand into a metal canister and pulled out a single sheet of papyrus covered in clear, protective plastic. Beneath its shiny cover, the parchment appeared fragile, yellow and extremely old.

The audience shuffled forwards in their seats as if trying to get closer to the paper. Everyone had heard the rumour, and they were desperate to know if it was true. Could this really be a letter written by Tutankhamun, the most famous pharaoh of them all? And, if it was, what had the boy king written? Would this finally solve the mystery of why he died so young?

In the audience, alongside some of the world's most important historians, sat two children, Maya and Joe. They were here, in Egypt, as guests of one of these historians, Professor Theo Smallwood. Maya was Theo's daughter, and Joe was his nephew.

"It can't be real," Maya whispered to Joe.

"Let's see what she says," replied Joe, squinting to make out the faint, spidery patterns of ink on the ancient document. He hoped very much that it was real.

"Ladies and gentlemen," said the woman. "Welcome to our brand-new research centre, here deep beneath the

Valley of the Kings, surrounded by the tombs of ancient Egypt's pharaohs. I am Professor Salma Boutros, and I'm sure that the document I am holding needs no introduction. The world's media has been talking about little else ever since it was discovered in a pit near King Tut's tomb three months ago. I hear it even has its own Twitter account!"

Amid the chuckles that followed this remark, a young voice shouted: "Was it really written by Tutankhamun?"

Joe was shocked and embarrassed to see it was Maya who had spoken. Other members of the audience glared disapprovingly at her, but Professor Boutros merely smiled.

"Indeed, that is the question on everybody's lips. So let me answer you with one word: yes!"

This was greeted by gasps and mutterings. Raising her voice above the hubbub, the professor continued: "The letter has been studied by experts from around the world, and they've all reached the same conclusion: it was most definitely written by King Tut himself."

"And what do the words say?" asked another member of the audience.

"Well…" Professor Boutros paused dramatically. "That is the most extraordinary thing of all. You see, this letter sheds new light on a 3,300-year-old mystery – it may help us understand why the young king died."

There were more gasps of astonishment, and this time the professor had to wait for the room to fall quiet again before resuming. "The letter," she said, "has been dated to January 1327 BC, close to the time of Tut's death. It reads as follows...."

She lowered her gaze to the letter and adjusted her spectacles. Joe felt prickles of anticipation on the back of his neck as he waited for her to speak....

"To Ay, my Grand Vizier," she read. "Thus speaks your king, Tutankhamun. As you know, in recent times, our kingdom has been struck by many disasters. First, my precious jewel was stolen – the jewel that gave me the protection of the gods. Then we suffered plague and poor harvests. And now I, your king, have fallen sick. Soon, my spirit will begin its journey to the Next World.

"I fear for Egypt when I am gone. For the sake of our kingdom, you must find the jewel and restore it to me or my successor. Do this, Ay, and I promise your spirit will dwell in the Land of the Gods forever."

A stunned silence followed these words. Professor Boutros looked up from the paper. "A stolen jewel, a series of disasters, a sick young king. Are they connected? It's so intriguing, wouldn't you agree, ladies and gentlemen? Who stole the jewel, and why? And what, if anything, does that have to do with the king's illness? This letter raises many fascinating questions. Sadly, we may never learn the answers…."

Joe felt a nudge from Maya. "Are you thinking what I'm thinking?" she asked.

"No," he said firmly. "I am definitely *not* thinking that."

What Maya was thinking was that she and Joe *could* learn the answers to these questions. They might even be able to recover the jewel and save King Tut from an early death. This was because Joe owned a timephone – a device that could take the two of them anywhere in history.

They had already been on several adventures to the past, righting wrongs and solving mysteries. Yet for some reason, the idea of using it to travel to ancient Egypt made Joe nervous.

"Don't you feel sorry for poor King Tut?' asked Maya.

Joe snorted. "Of course I do, but…." He tried to think of what was bothering him. "But this would mean travelling thousands of years into the past. I don't even know if the timephone has enough power to send us that far *and* bring us back."

"It's never let us down before," said Maya.

"That's true," said Joe, "but there's another thing. Tut is famous – *really* famous. I'm not sure we should be messing around with history like this. It might change everything."

"Where's your sense of adventure, Joe? You've been given this phone for a reason – well, maybe this is it!"

Joe was still hesitant.

"Come on, cuz, let's talk about this outside," Maya persisted. "I need some air."

Joe followed her out of the auditorium, up some steps and through a swing door. They emerged into a dry, dusty valley, surrounded by barren, limestone hills – the Valley of the Kings. Cut into the base of these hills were the entrances to the tombs.

Joe could see a coach full of tourists approaching along a dusty road. Another coach had stopped at the visitor centre, and tourists were climbing out and pointing at things and taking selfies.

Suddenly, he was filled with an immense curiosity. He wanted to meet the people who had created these tombs that the world was still marvelling at thousands of years later. He wasn't sure if finding the jewel and helping Tut was a good idea, but… he had to admit he wanted to go back there.

"Okay," he said to Maya. "Let's do this."

She gave a little whoop of delight. "I knew you wouldn't be able to resist, Joe!"

They ducked behind an ancient stone statue and Joe took the timephone out of his pocket. The screen lit up:

Hello Joe Smallwood.
Which time would you like to visit?

He twirled the date dials on the screen all the way back to January 1327 BC. According to Professor Boutros, that was the month the king had written the letter.

He felt Maya's hand on his arm, and pressed "Go".

The scene around them dissolved into a swirling grey, as if a silent dust storm had risen out of the ground and enveloped them. For quite a long time they stood within this churning cloud as the phone sucked them backwards through the centuries.

Finally, the cloud dispersed and they found themselves gazing on a very different scene. The hills were still there, as were many of the tomb entrances. But the stone statues and carvings were new, as if recently made. There were no buses, no roads, railings or signs, and no visitor centre. It was a very bleak, dead place. They seemed to be the only things alive in the entire valley.

And then, quite suddenly, music burst upon their ears, echoing all around them.

It was the sound of women singing in joyful rhythm, accompanied by drums, rattles, bells and hand claps.

Joe and Maya spun around to see a large crowd of people all dressed in white. They were gathered before the entrance of King Tut's tomb. In the middle of the throng, some women were dancing. Their gold bracelets flashed in the sun as they waved their arms about. They were performing to a young man who wore a magnificent headdress and jewelled collar and belt. Joe started. Could that be King Tut? … It *was!* Joe was sure of it. And the men surrounding him, also in decorative collars and belts, had to be his courtiers.

"Just look at us," Maya suddenly sniggered.

Joe wondered what she was talking about. Then he looked down and saw that he was wearing a linen tunic and kilt. It felt cool and comfortable in the heat. Maya was in a pleated, ankle-length dress of the same material.

"Let's find out what's happening," she said.

There was something odd about the way Maya was speaking. It didn't sound as if she was speaking English – yet Joe found he could understand every word she said.

"Hey," he said. "I think we're speaking ancient Egyptian...."

"You what?" Maya laughed. "That's crazy! I LOVE time travel! Come on, let's go and join the party."

Chapter 2

A Necklace

They sneaked closer, and slipped into the rear of the crowd surrounding the dancers and the king. Taking care not to draw attention to themselves, they gently threaded their way through the mass of people, moving ever closer to the middle.

At last they found themselves standing some ten paces from the king. By now, Joe was sweating – overcome by the crush of the crowd, the noise and the singing – yet filled with excitement. Tutankhamun had been world famous since 1922, when

Howard Carter discovered his tomb. He'd been the subject of loads of exhibitions, books and TV programmes. And now here they were, face to face with the man himself. He looked so young – not much older than Joe or Maya. He also appeared weak from illness as he leaned upon his richly decorated staff. Servants carrying large ostrich-feather fans wafted cool air over him.

Suddenly, Joe was barged aside as a man burst out of the crowd and made straight for the king. He threw himself to the ground before him.

The dancers stopped in confusion, and the music came to a discordant halt.

"What is the meaning of this?" roared one of Tut's courtiers – a tall, thin man with a narrow beard dangling from his chin. "You may be Chief of Police, Mahu, but that does not give you the right to interrupt a royal ceremony. Are you not aware that we are celebrating the completion of our beloved king's tomb?"

"I humbly beg your forgiveness, Lord Ay," cried Mahu, "but a discovery has been made." He raised his head a little to look upon King Tut. "A possession of yours, O Great King – a very precious possession… has been recovered."

Mahu reached inside his leather bag and pulled out a shiny metal object.

Lord Ay reached down and plucked it from the police chief's outstretched hand. He held it up for everyone to see. It was an ornate gold necklace encrusted with colourful stones. But something seemed to be missing from it – there was a large, oval-shaped hollow at its centre.

"The jewel!" gasped Tut when he saw it. "Where is the jewel?"

"I… I don't know, Lord of the World!" spluttered Mahu. "It was missing when we found the necklace."

"I care nothing for the necklace," the king sighed. "That is not precious to me at all." He leaned closer to the policeman. "But I need that jewel, Mahu. It was forged in the rays of Ra, God of the Sun. It gives me His blessing and protection. It is the symbol of my royal authority. Without it I have become weak, and I fear I shall soon die."

"Have hope, O Heavenly Prince," said Ay. "We have recovered the necklace, so the jewel cannot be far away." He turned to Mahu. "Where did you find this?"

"In the home of a young priest…. A man by the name of Bek. He is now under arrest."

"Bring him before us," Ay ordered.

"Yes, my lord." Mahu rose to his feet and gave a nod to some guards. The guards had hold of a rope-bound prisoner. They dragged him before Ay and threw him to his knees.

Ay stared menacingly at the prisoner. "Are you Bek?"

"Yes, Lord Ay," said the young man in a shaking voice. Joe thought he looked even younger than Tut – a boy of no more than fifteen.

"Did you steal this necklace?"

"No, Lord Ay. Please believe me."

"Then can you explain why it was found at your house?"

"I cannot, Lord Ay."

"Where is the jewel, Bek?" asked Tut.

"I don't know, O King of Kings," quavered Bek. "I have never seen this necklace before. And I know nothing of its jewel."

Tut bashed his staff on the ground in frustration.

"He is most certainly guilty, Your Majesty," said Ay. "Tell us where the jewel is, boy, and we may let you live. If not, you will be thrown to the crocodiles in the Nile."

"Sire, I… I *swear* I don't know where it is."

"You have until sunrise tomorrow to make your confession," said Ay coldly. "Mahu, take him to the royal dungeon."

Joe and Maya watched as the frightened young man was hauled away.

"Do you think he did it?" Maya asked.

"No," said Joe. "I think he's been set up."

"How do you know?"

Joe shrugged. "Just a feeling."

"We need to try and get into the royal dungeon, so we can question him – find out for sure if he's guilty or innocent."

"That might be difficult," said Joe.

The music and dancing had started up again. The crowd sang and clapped along with its rhythms, but neither Ay nor Tut looked in the mood for celebrating.

Joe whispered into Maya's ear: "Don't you think there's something quite suspicious about Lord Ay – the way he was so quick to decide Bek is guilty. Maybe *he's* the thief."

Maya stared at him. "Why would Ay steal a jewel? He looks wealthy enough to buy his own."

"You heard what Tut said. He who wears the jewel has the blessing of Ra. Maybe Ay wants to be pharaoh. He could have stolen the necklace, taken out the jewel, then ordered his men to plant the necklace on Bek."

Maya nodded slowly. "Hmm… I guess that's possible. Tut looks pretty sick. Even if I didn't know the future, I'd reckon he isn't going to be around much longer. Ay's probably thinking this is his chance."

"Why don't we try and get jobs as palace servants so we can keep an eye on Ay?" suggested Joe.

Maya giggled. "An eye on Ay. I like it!" Then she became serious. "No, I still think we need to try and talk to Bek. He's going to be killed tomorrow morning, so there's not much time. Perhaps he can tell us something that will help us prove his innocence."

"But how on earth do you suggest we do that?" Joe asked.

For once, Maya didn't have an answer.

Chapter 3

Saving a Life

The music faded and the ceremony came to an end. The royal procession began slowly winding its way up a path that led out of the valley. Joe and Maya tagged along behind.

Soon, the dry brown landscape gave way to lush grassland and palm trees. Then they saw, through the morning mist, the blue expanse of the River Nile. On the far side stood the high walls of a great city.

"Thebes!" gasped Joe.

Moored below them on the riverbank

were two luxurious barges. They had enormous curving prows and hulls painted in gleaming gold, red and blue. Eight oarsmen sat in each barge, ready to take the king and his companions back across the river to the royal palace.

King Tut, along with his courtiers, servants and dancers, took their places in the first barge. The king looked hunched and frail as he seated himself beneath the shade of a gilded canopy.

Chief of Police Mahu boarded the second barge, along with the guards and the prisoner, Bek, his wrists still bound with rope.

"Come on," whispered Maya, making her way towards the second barge. "We need to stay close to Bek."

Joe hesitated. "They'll never let us on," he predicted.

"The trick is to act confidently – as if you belong there," said Maya, and she marched up and planted herself in the line of people waiting to board the barge.

Reluctantly, Joe followed.

The chief guard eyed them suspiciously as they climbed up the ramp. But, to Joe's immense relief, he didn't say anything.

The moorings were cast off and the oarsmen began rowing the barges east across the still waters of the river.

Joe still had no idea what they would do once they arrived in Thebes. It was all very well thinking they could become palace servants, but how would they actually go about doing that? And if they tried to sneak into the royal dungeon to talk to Bek, they could end up as prisoners themselves – once someone noticed them. They might even face execution!

He had to think of a plan, and quickly, before they reached the other side of the river.

He leaned back against the rail and gazed at the dark blue water, waiting for inspiration to strike. Suddenly, a flash of movement beneath the surface caught his eye. There was something big and green down there. Then the barge rocked violently.

Water splashed into Joe's eyes. When he opened them, he saw a huge reptile rising out of the river right near where he was sitting. Its knobbly scales were like plates of armour. Its enormous jaws were spread wide, revealing a long row of sharp, yellow teeth.

A crocodile!

It crashed down on the side of the barge, tipping it sideways. Screams erupted in the boat. Joe felt Maya slam into him as everyone slid towards the water. Joe grabbed onto the side of the boat to avoid falling in. Others scrambled for something to hold onto. One man was not so quick to react, and he tumbled with a splash into the river. Then the crocodile slid back into the water, and the barge righted itself.

"Help!" cried the man who had fallen overboard.

Joe was shocked to see it was Bek. Because his wrists were tied he couldn't swim, and he was frantically kicking just to keep himself afloat. The crocodile was circling him just below the surface, getting closer and closer.

Then came another splash as someone from the barge dived in. Joe watched the small figure streak through the water towards the floundering Bek. A terrible jolt went through him when he saw who it was.

Maya!

Was she crazy?

He had to do something to save her. Joe was a rubbish swimmer. What could he do?

He watched helplessly as she reached Bek and began pulling him back to safety. But the crocodile had positioned itself between them and the barge. The reptile was drifting motionless in the water. Only its eyes were visible above the surface, its jaws slightly open, waiting for them to come within reach.

Two of the rowers were thrashing their oars at the huge beast, but to no avail.

Then Joe spotted something in the hands of one of the guards. Before he could react, Joe snatched the man's bow and plucked an arrow from his quiver. He might not be much of a swimmer, but Joe knew all about archery, having practised it in the forests near his home in Dorset.

Maya was swimming backwards towards the barge, kicking with her legs while holding onto Bek, keeping his head above water. She didn't see that the crocodile was almost upon her. Its jaws widened, ready to strike, as Joe struggled to fit the notch of the arrow onto the bowstring.

Finally managing it, he drew the bow, aimed, and fired. The arrow struck the reptile in the neck, and it jerked wildly. Its jaws snapped shut… on air.

Then the huge creature plunged deep beneath the water and disappeared from view.

Seconds later, guards were helping Maya and Bek on board. Joe was shaking as he handed the bow and arrow back to the guard.

He stared at the now-dripping Maya.

"Thank you, cuz," she whispered.

She, too, he noticed, was shivering.

"I thought you'd had it," he croaked.

"I am grateful to you, young lady," gasped the exhausted Bek. "You have granted me one more day of life."

"Longer than that, I hope," Maya told him.

Bek stared at her, puzzled. Before she had a chance to explain, a voice behind them barked: "Identify yourselves!"

They turned and saw it was Mahu, the chief of police.

Joe froze, unable to think of a reply. Luckily, Maya had a knack for thinking on her feet.

"I'm Maya, a priestess in training," she said. "Joe here works at the palace."

"Joe… Maya, what strange names," Mahu glared at them for a moment. Then his face relaxed into a smile. "You acted bravely, both of you."

Joe could breathe again. Maya had bought them some time – though surely her story would unravel once they reached the far shore.

At length, they docked at the harbour of Thebes. As they disembarked, a servant from the royal barge bustled up to Joe and Maya. "The king wishes to see you," he informed them.

Now we're in trouble! fretted Joe.

He and Maya approached the young pharaoh, who was standing on the quayside surrounded by his entourage. They lay down before him as they'd seen Mahu do earlier.

"Get up! Get up!" cried Tut. "I want to see your faces."

The children clambered to their feet.

"I saw everything!" Tut exclaimed

excitedly. "The attack by the crocodile, and your rescue of the prisoner. Lord Ay thinks it was a judgement of the gods. He says you should have left Bek to die. But I don't agree. I think what you did was incredible!"

Joe was amazed and delighted to hear this from the king. He was also pleased to see that Tut was looking a little more lively than before.

"I want you to be my personal servant," said Tut, pointing at Joe. "I could do with having someone as brave as you around."

"King of the Universe, are you sure…?" interjected Ay.

"Of course I'm sure!" said Tut. "And as for you, young lady. I want you to be… um…."

The king of the universe seemed to have

run out of inspiration.

Then Mahu spoke up: "O Lord of Earth and Sky, she's training to be a priestess. With Bek gone, there's now a vacancy at the Temple of Anhur. Her courage makes me think she'd make a perfect replacement."

"I quite agree," said Tut.

"Thanks, Lord of… um… Everything," said Maya, looking flushed.

"Follow me, boy!" Tut said to Joe.

"And you come with me," Mahu said to Maya.

The two young time-travellers barely had a chance to say goodbye to each other.

"I'll try and get into the dungeon," Maya hissed at Joe.

"And I'll keep an eye on…" began Joe. But he was already being led away.

Chapter 4

A Suspect

Maya watched as Tut reclined himself upon the cushions of a curtained litter. Four servants, Joe included, hoisted it up and carried it through a huge pair of gates into the city.

"This way," said Mahu, and Maya followed him towards another, smaller gate. Behind them came the guards, and Bek. Mahu took a large ring from his finger and flashed it at the soldiers guarding the gate. With a bow, they immediately opened it for him.

Thebes was a beautiful city of broad avenues lined with palm trees and statues of sphinxes and other mythical creatures. There were enormous pillared temples, artificial lakes and fountains. Amid the crowds of civilians were soldiers carrying spears and dressed in gleaming, gold-plated armour. They guarded the arched entrances to the royal precincts of the city. As Mahu approached them, he would show them his ring, and they would open the gates.

I need that ring! thought Maya.

Eventually, they arrived at the royal dungeon – a grim-looking building with high walls and barred windows. Here, Mahu once again displayed his ring, and handed Bek over to the prison guards.

Maya took care to memorise the dungeon's location as she and Mahu continued on their journey.

Reaching the Temple of Anhur, they entered a shaded courtyard. Maya noticed that Mahu had not yet replaced the ring on his finger. It was still in his hand.

Seizing her chance, she deliberately tripped over a loose floor tile. She tumbled into Mahu, propelling him into a small pile of earthenware jars. They crashed to the ground as water, oil and shards of shattered pottery spilled out onto the floor… along with the ring belonging to the police chief. As he rose, grumbling, to his feet, she nimbly retrieved the ring, slipping it into her hand. Annoyed with her, and embarrassed about the mess he'd created, Mahu failed to notice the theft.

Unfortunately, this 'accident' did not endear her to the temple's chief priestess, who came running out when she heard the commotion.

"Are you sure she's suitable for this sacred job?" she asked Mahu.

"I am," said Mahu, "and so is the king!"

* * *

Maya realized pretty quickly that being an ancient Egyptian priestess was not half as glamorous as it sounded. Her duties included lighting incense in bronze vessels, scrubbing stone floors, washing the golden statue of Anhur, and placing offerings of scented oil and water before it – all under the watchful gaze of a very suspicious-looking chief priestess.

She wished she'd leave her alone so she could escape. Time was running out before Bek's execution and she needed to speak to him.

Her chance came in the early afternoon. The chief priestess told her to sweep the floor of the temple's main hall, then left on some other business.

Wasting no time, Maya flung down the bundle of twigs that served as a broom. Then she raced out through the courtyard and into the street. Within minutes, she was back at the royal dungeon.

Maya had learned early in life that a confident approach could get you a long way with grown-ups, be they schoolteachers or prison guards. She strode up to the man at the entrance and flashed Mahu's ring at him, making sure he saw the pattern engraved into its surface.

"Mahu sent me," she said. "I have orders to question the prisoner, Bek, about the king's jewel. We need to know what he did with it."

The man frowned at her, then took another long look at the ring. "Now why would the chief of police entrust a young maid like you with such a task?" he demanded.

"Because *I* know how to get to the truth," she replied, quick as a snake. "And the truth is, you have no future, unless you let me in right this minute. Or would you like me to tell Lord Ay that you barred my way?"

The mention of Ay seemed to do the trick. The guard gulped and pushed open the door. "Wait here," he said, before disappearing inside the building.

At that moment, Maya heard a loud and familiar voice coming through an open window to her left. She could see Mahu looking very angry indeed. He was shouting instructions to a soldier: "Now my ring with the royal seal has gone missing. And that girl, the young 'priestess' has vanished. What is going on around here? Find her and bring her back to me!"

Maya spun around. The prison guard had reappeared. Luckily, he had missed Mahu's outburst. "This man will escort you to Bek," he said to Maya.

She hurried through the door and followed the other guard along a gloomy corridor lined with cell doors. Eventually, they came to Bek's cell. The guard slipped a large wooden key into a lock and opened the door.

It smelled pretty grim inside the cell. Bek, who was lying on a rough straw mattress, started up in surprise when she entered. He looked wretched, his eyes red from crying, yet he appeared happy to see her.

"You!" he said. "The girl who saved me from the crocodile."

"I'd like to save you from execution if I can." Maya whispered this, aware that the guard was waiting just outside.

"But how?" asked Bek. "And why are you doing this for me?"

"Because I don't believe you're guilty."

Bek's eyes, for the first time, seemed to shine with hope. "I'm not!" he breathed. "I never stole that necklace, or the jewel."

Maya nodded. "I know. But I need to find proof of your innocence, so we can convince Ay and the king." Again, she glanced over her shoulder. "We haven't got much time. I stole Mahu's ring to get in here, and now they're out searching for me. You *must* tell me everything."

Bek furrowed his brow. "I went to see my father last night. I go there whenever I can, because he gets so lonely and finds it hard to sleep since my mother died. For most of the night, we talked and played *senet* – that's a board game, as I'm sure you know. I got back home this morning just before dawn, and I found the necklace on my table. As I picked it up, guards suddenly swarmed into my house and arrested me."

"Then you have a witness who can speak up for you," said Maya excitedly. "I'll go and speak to your father now."

Bek shook his head sadly. "I'm afraid he is old and his memory is not good. He may not even remember I was there…."

"Well, was there anyone else who saw you last night?"

Again, Bek started to shake his head. Then suddenly he became very still and thoughtful. "Wait!" he said. "There *was* someone. As I was returning home, I saw a woman walking in the other direction.

She wore a hood and her face was in shadow, but it looked – I know this sounds impossible – it looked like Queen Ankhe, the wife of our great king.

"I thought perhaps she had come to pray at the temple. I live just next door to it, you see. Perhaps she did not want to be seen by anyone, so she came very early in the morning. As we passed each other, our eyes met. I saw a mole on her cheek… that's how I knew it was her. Then she walked on… Do you think that maybe Queen Ankhe will be my witness?"

Maya frowned. "I think that Queen Ankhe might be the culprit. Don't you see? She didn't go to the temple. She went to your house and planted the necklace there. She wanted you to take the blame for her theft!"

Chapter 5

A Dangerous Rivalry

"I hope Queen Ankhe is in a better mood today," Tut said to Joe. "She blames me for everything, you know. Now her beloved cat's gone missing, and she thinks I got rid of it. She won't speak to me."

The king lay back on his bed and stared grumpily at the ceiling.

"I admit I've sometimes felt like strangling that pampered pet, but of course I never actually would…."

They were in the king's bedchamber. Tut had insisted on coming straight here upon reaching the palace, and Joe had helped him to bed, even though it was the middle of the day. Joe stared at all the luxury on display – the golden chalices, masks, weapons, statues and jewellery. This young man had everything he could possibly desire. He was a god to his people. Yet he seemed so weak and unhappy.

Joe wished he could help.

"I can speak to the queen if you wish, my lord," he offered.

Tut nodded. "Yes, that would be good. Could you tell her–"

"Why don't you tell me yourself?" came a shrill voice from the doorway. Joe turned to see a young woman dressed in a beautifully embroidered white gown striding into the room.

Tut raised himself up on his cushions. "My queen!" he gasped.

"Have you found Bes yet?" demanded Ankhe. She was a petite young woman with big dark eyes that flashed with anger. Joe couldn't help noticing the rather large mole on her cheek.

"I have twenty men out searching for her," said Tut. "They have orders not to come back until she is found. I would be out there looking for the poor creature myself if I were not so ill."

"I doubt that very much!" she sneered. "What would be the point? You and I both know you killed her."

"I–I…" Tut stuttered.

"Just like you murdered my mother, Queen Nefertiti!" snarled Ankhe. "You kill everything I love. Admit it, husband!"

"I did *not* murder your mother!" cried Tut, horrified.

"I think you did! You wanted to be king.

She stood in your way. So you had her killed! And now the gods are punishing you with this illness."

Joe was astonished by this accusation. If Ankhe believed Tut had killed her mother, then perhaps *she*, not Ay, was behind the plot to bring him down. She could have stolen the jewel to damage his authority. She could even be behind Tut's illness. Perhaps she was poisoning him?

"That's not true!" protested Tut. "I felt nothing but love and respect for your mother…."

"Just find my Bes!" spat Ankhe, and she turned on her heel and left the room.

Tut sighed. "The cat is just the latest disaster, Joe…. Everything's been going wrong since I lost that jewel."

"We'll find the cat *and* the jewel, my lord," Joe assured him.

Tut smiled ruefully. "I hope you're right – and I hope I live to see the day. I'm dying, you know."

"You'll get better. You just need rest."

"There's no time for rest," said the king. "While I still have breath in my body, I must try and find that jewel. Without it, this kingdom will fall. I need to write to Lord Ay. Fetch me my scribe…. Ah, no. Forget that. The queen dismissed him yesterday. Apparently, he said something to offend her. You'll have to be my scribe, Joe. You can read and write, can't you?"

"Yes, but–" Joe started.

Tut pointed to a table in the corner of the room. "You'll find papyrus and a reed pen over there."

"My lord, I–"

Joe didn't have a clue how to write ancient Egyptian.

"Do it!" commanded his king. "While I still have the strength."

Not daring to disobey, Joe hurried to the table and seated himself there. He unfurled a blank scroll and dipped a pen in the inkwell.

"To Ay, my Grand Vizier…" began Tut.

Joe lowered the pen to the parchment. He would have to write the words in English. What else could he do? Tut would soon realize that his new scribe was useless, and he'd be sacked.

But to Joe's astonishment, what flowed out from his pen were not English words, but strange symbols. Of course! They were hieroglyphics. And Joe found he could write them effortlessly – *and* understand what they meant.

"Thus speaks your king, Tutankhamun," continued Tut. "As you know, in recent times, our kingdom has been struck by many disasters...."

With a shiver, Joe suddenly realized what he was writing. This was *the* letter! The letter that thousands of years in the future would become world famous. He'd seen it himself – that tattered ancient document wrapped in protective plastic. Who would have guessed that he of all people had written it! Joe's head began to spin....

"Did you get all that," Tut asked him.

Joe finished writing the last few words, and nodded.

"Good!" said Tut. "Now give it to the man outside and tell him to take it to Lord Ay."

"Yes, my lord."

Joe rolled up the scroll, bowed and departed the bedchamber. He handed the scroll to the messenger outside. Then, on a whim, he decided to follow him. He was curious to see how Lord Ay took the news that the king might be dying. Would he be happy or sad? If he was happy, then maybe Joe had been right in his first suspicion, and Lord Ay was behind the plot.

Stealthily, he followed the man out of the royal apartment and into a beautiful garden. He trailed the messenger out across a large open space with an artificial lake at its centre. On the far side of the lake stood Lord Ay's apartment.

Joe hid behind a statue and watched the man enter, then leave a few moments later.

Once the messenger was out of sight, Joe climbed the steps to the apartment entrance and peeked in. Ay was standing at the far end of the room with his back to

Joe. He was leaning against an arched entrance leading to another room, talking to someone in there.

Joe took his opportunity and scampered silently across the room towards a large wooden storage chest. He opened the lid. It was half filled with linen garments, on top of which sat a beautiful golden belt studded with precious stones. Luckily, there was just enough space in the chest for Joe, so he hastily clambered inside and closed the lid, leaving a tiny gap to see through.

"Tey, I've received this letter from the king," Ay was saying to the other person. "He tells me he's dying. He wants me to find the missing jewel – for the sake of the kingdom."

From his new position inside the chest, Joe could see Tey, the woman being addressed. She was seated before a polished bronze mirror, using a tiny brush to apply a dark cosmetic to her eyelashes.

She turned to face Ay, her mouth hanging open in surprise, and Joe noticed that one of her front teeth was missing.

"Did he seem as if he was dying when you saw him at the ceremony this morning, husband?" she asked.

"Yes," said Ay, "which means we haven't got long. There will be a power struggle when he dies. General Horem, commander of the army, will want to take control. Before he can do that, I must declare myself pharaoh, and obtain oaths of loyalty from the council of ministers."

As he was saying this, there came a pounding of heavy footsteps outside. Joe swivelled his gaze in time to see a huge man enter the apartment. The visitor had a gleaming bald head, thick lips and dark eyebrows. His gold-plated armour left his muscular brown arms exposed. From the frown and the tightly clenched fists, Joe guessed he was angry.

Ay turned to face his guest. "General! To what do I owe the pleasure?"

"Cut out the charm, Ay, it won't work on me!" snarled Horem, advancing on the grand vizier. "I know what you're up to. The king's jewel has gone missing. You've pinned the blame on some young priest, but I'm sure you were behind it. And now the king is sick. Admit it, you're planning to take over the kingdom."

Lord Ay laughed at this. "Why, General, I could make exactly the same accusation against you. Everyone knows how much you crave power. If Bek didn't steal the jewel then it could only have been you.

As commander of the army, and guardian of the royal treasury, you would have had access to it. Whereas I...."

"*You*, Ay, have access to the king. I would not be surprised if you were poisoning him!"

For the first time, a flush of anger appeared on Lord Ay's smooth cheeks. "I love the king," he said with dangerous quietness. "I have served him loyally, as I did his father before him. I am deeply offended by your accusation, general, and I insist that you withdraw it."

Horem glowered and reached for his sword. Joe wondered if the two men were about to have a fight.

Then Tey stepped back into the room.

"General," she said sweetly, kissing him on both cheeks. "How nice of you to visit. Would you care for a fig?"

She picked up a bowl of ripe, juicy figs and offered it to him. When he declined, she shrugged and took one herself.

"It was your birthday yesterday, wasn't it, General?" she smiled after taking a bite. "I have a present for you. Now, where did I put it…? Ah, yes, in there…."

Then to Joe's horror, she strode over to the chest….

Chapter 6

Accusations

After giving it some thought, Maya decided that her best course of action would be to go to Bek's house and see if she could find any evidence there of Ankhe's guilt. It was late afternoon by the time she sneaked out of the royal dungeon. Bek was due to be executed at dawn tomorrow, so time was running out.

Bek had told her he lived next door to the Temple of Anhur. Maya moved quickly through the streets, keeping to the shadows, aware that Police Chief Mahu's soldiers were still out looking for her. After skirting the walls of the temple, she turned a corner and came in sight of a small, simple house, exactly as Bek had described. Some children were playing skittles near the front step, trying to knock down some tall stones with a wooden ball. As Maya approached them, she heard the sound of marching footsteps behind her. She glanced over her shoulder and caught a glint of armour and spears.

Soldiers!

Maya lowered her head and quickly headed over to where the children were playing. She kneeled down among them, looking – she hoped – like just another kid.

"Hey, that's ours!" complained a boy, when she scooped up their wooden ball. Maya winked at him and tossed the ball towards a skittle, knocking it over.

The soldiers hesitated a moment, and she felt their eyes upon her.

Then they marched on by.

Relieved, she got back to her feet and hurried into the house.

The interior was very dark, so Maya left the door ajar. The shaft of sunlight illuminated a modest dwelling. There was a mat of woven straw on the floor, a flimsy ladder leading to the roof, a wooden stool, a tub for washing in, a bed, a chest and a small table where Bek said he'd discovered Tut's necklace. Maya went over to the table. The surface was bare, apart from a bowl of purple figs. There was nothing on the floor around the table. Ankhe (if it was she) had taken care to leave no trace of her visit.

Maya dropped to her knees to look beneath the bed. Perhaps something had rolled under there. Apart from the chamber pot, she saw nothing. It was too dark, so she reached under and felt around. Her hand touched something small and soft.

Maya drew an excited breath. *Could it be a purse or glove dropped by Queen Ankhe?*

She pulled it out and held it up to the light – then heaved a disappointed sigh.

It was a fig!

Sticky red juice dripped onto her finger. *Yuck!* A bite had been taken out of it. Clearly Bek (or Queen Ankhe) didn't believe in throwing things in the bin – assuming they even had bins in ancient Egypt.

Suddenly the door opened wide. Maya stuffed the fig in her pocket, just as light, and soldiers, flooded the room.

"Stand up, Maya!" ordered Mahu. "I'm arresting you for deserting your temple and your priestly duties!" Then he spotted something gleaming on her finger and his face turned pink with rage. "And for stealing my ring with the royal seal!"

* * *

Joe cowered helplessly inside the chest as Tey came closer. He watched her hand reach down and grasp the rim of the lid and he cringed, waiting for the inevitable exposure.

But her hand didn't lift the lid. It froze for a second, then let go.

What had happened?

That was when Joe noticed new people entering Ay's house. Police Chief Mahu came first, followed by several guards, and… *Maya!*

Joe was pleased to see her, but also concerned. The guards were holding her. She was under arrest.

Mahu read out the charges against her to Lord Ay. "This girl, who calls herself Maya, ran away from the temple where she was supposed to be training to be a priestess. She stole my official ring, and was later found lurking suspiciously inside the home of the convicted thief, Bek–"

"Bek is not the thief!" interjected Maya. "I was there trying to prove his innocence. I wanted to find evidence left by the real thief."

"And who do you think the real thief is?" asked General Horem, frowning at Ay.

"Yes, who?" demanded Ay, glaring back at Horem.

While everyone waited for Maya to answer, Joe saw Tey suddenly dart closer to Horem and slip something into his pocket. *What could she have put there?* Joe's mind grew dizzy with the possibilities.

Could Ay's wife and the head of the army be secretly in league to overthrow Tut?

Maya hesitated, seemingly in two minds about whether to reveal what she knew. "I have a theory," she said eventually. "But I need more evidence to back it up." She gazed at the faces surrounding her. "Does anyone know where Queen Ankhe was last night?"

There was a gasp from all those in the room.

"Now I've heard quite enough!" cried Lord Ay.

"So have I," said Horem. "The girl is clearly mad if she thinks she can bring the queen into this! I must go. Lord Ay, you will be hearing from me again very soon!"

With that, Horem left.

Joe crouched frustrated in the chest, desperately wishing he could follow

Horem to find out what Tey had planted in his pocket.

"Making such outrageous allegations against the queen sounds a lot like treason to me," declared Mahu. "What is your verdict on this girl, Lord Ay? Execution?"

The grand vizier was about to reply when a servant suddenly rushed into the room.

He bowed to Ay. "My Lord, you must come quickly."

"What is it?"

"The king has taken a turn for the worse. He is vomiting and constantly thirsty. The pupils of his eyes are wide and he struggles to see. He babbles of strange visions. I fear he may be close to death."

"I shall come immediately!" declared Ay, and he rushed out after the servant, closely followed by Tey, Mahu and the guards, still holding onto Maya.

Chapter 7

A Deadly Poison

As soon as they were gone, Joe leapt out of the chest. He was desperate to chase after Horem, but something made him hesitate. It was the guard's description of Tut's condition – vomiting, thirst, dilated pupils, blurred vision, hallucinations. It reminded Joe of something he'd read in a detective story once. They were the exact symptoms of a poisoning. But which poison?

Joe tried to think. There was a clue, he remembered, in the title of the book – The

Night's Deadly Shade. That was it! The poison was deadly nightshade, also known as belladonna. He should go and tell Tut's doctor. Then again, it wouldn't help Tut, unless the doctor knew of an antidote.

Joe stepped out onto the front porch of Lord Ay's villa. The sky was dimming. Soon it would be night. He watched as Ay and the others made their way hurriedly around the lake towards the king's apartment.

He could tell Tut's doctor later about his poisoning theory, he decided. And his cousin always found a way to wriggle out of trouble. He was sure Maya wouldn't be captive for long.

What mattered more right now was saving Bek. At dawn, the young priest would be executed. Joe had to devote the time that remained to proving his innocence.

He needed to continue with his detective work, and that meant finding out what Tey had put in General Horem's pocket.

Looking in the other direction, Joe saw in the distance the muscular figure of Horem striding towards an enormous pillared hall. Silently, he hurried after him.

When he reached the hall, he mounted the steps two at a time. The pillars towered high above him. He felt tiny, like an insect, as he moved cautiously between them and into the shadow of the vast hall.

At the far end, in the flickering glow of torchlight, he saw Horem, head bowed, kneeling before a giant statue. The statue was of a seated figure, taller than a double-decker bus, with the body of a human and the head of a bird. Keeping to the shadows, Joe crept closer, until he was within earshot of the general.

"O Horus, God of War," he heard Horem chant. "I have always been your most loyal servant. Grant me strength in the coming contest with Lord Ay. Give me the power to defeat him!"

The general's hands were clasped tightly together. His muscles rippled and there were sweat beads on his gleaming scalp. "Son of Isis and Osiris, I need a sign," he cried. "Some small sign to give me proof of your favour!"

Suddenly, Horem jerked upright. He dipped his head and stared with wide eyes at the pocket in his kilt.

Joe watched, fascinated, as a dazed Horem reached inside the pocket and took out… a golden key.

The general studied it for a moment before his fist closed tightly round it.

"Thank you, Horus," he smiled. Then he

rose to his feet and began walking swiftly back along the hall.

Joe darted out of sight just in time. He followed at a distance as Horem strode out of the hall and down the steps. Night had fallen, and moonlight twinkled like ghostly silver upon the still surface of the lake. On its shores stood a squat, sturdy-looking building with no windows and a huge door as golden as the key.

From behind a thicket of palms, Joe observed Horem approach the building. The general was about to push the key into the lock of the door when a figure suddenly raced up to him from the direction of the king's apartment.

"General!" cried the figure, and Joe recognized him as Mahu, chief of police.

Mahu stopped in surprise when he saw what was in Horem's hand.

"The key!" he gasped. "You found it!"

"Yes," said Horem. "Just now, it appeared mysteriously in my pocket. I believe it's a sign from Horus. I'm not yet certain what it means, but I know that we will be victorious, Mahu."

"I hope so, General," said Mahu. "I'm afraid the king is close to death."

Horem stiffened at this news. "Then the battle is upon us. I've no doubt Ay is making his preparations. We must make ours. Let's go now to the barracks and speak to the soldiers."

Joe watched them both march quickly away, and he kicked the sand in frustration. He'd been about to discover why the key was so important and what lay behind that door – then Mahu had showed up. Now he'd probably never find out.

Joe could think of no reason to follow them to the barracks, so he began making his way, somewhat dejectedly, back to the king's apartment.

To get there he had to go through the royal garden. It was a dim green underworld of dense foliage, palms and thick-stemmed creepers. To the croak of frogs and the hiss of water trickling over rocks, he made his way along the winding mossy path.

Through the trees up ahead, he could see torches illuminating the entrance to the king's apartment, and he could hear guards out on patrol. A couple of them had entered the garden and were prodding their spears through the undergrowth as if searching for something.

A low whistle sounded from a nearby tree, making him jump with fright. He quickened his pace.

"Joe!" hissed a voice.

He stopped. "Maya?"

Peering into the gloom, he saw her beckoning to him, and ran over to where she was crouching by a tree.

"What are you doing here?" he gasped.

"Hiding," she grinned. "In all the fuss around the king, I managed to give the guards the slip. They really are quite useless. Now they're looking for me, so make sure you don't give me away." She tugged him further into her hiding place. "How are you getting on?" she whispered. "Have you discovered anything to help Bek?"

"Not really. What about you?"

"Not much – except that I think Ankhe is our thief. Bek said he saw a woman with a mole on her cheek near his house last night. But I'll need more proof than that before I can persuade Lord Ay that she's the guilty one."

Joe nodded. "Yeah, he didn't exactly sound convinced by your theory."

"How do you know?"

"I was there in his villa when you told him, hiding in the chest."

Maya clapped a hand over her mouth to stifle a giggle. "You sneaky little…." Then her eyes twinkled. "I'm impressed, cuz!"

"I think you might be right about Ankhe, too," said Joe. "She hates Tut – says he killed her mother, and her cat, though I don't believe he did. He seems too nice. Anyway, she's definitely got a motive for bringing him down."

"So, Ankhe's now our chief suspect," said Maya.

Chapter 8

Last Chances

Joe's attention had been caught by something nearby – a shrub growing in the shade of the tree where they were squatting. It had big purple flowers and shiny black berries. He recognized the plant from an illustration in a book he'd looked at in Castle Cranston, during their adventure last summer in medieval Scotland. The book had catalogued poisonous plants and their antidotes.

"This is belladonna," he breathed, staring at the plant.

"Bella-what?"

Joe gave a tight smile. "So I was right."

"Right about what exactly?" Maya looked confused, so Joe explained how he'd recognized the king's symptoms as being those of belladonna poisoning.

"I can remember the antidote, too," he muttered. The medieval book had described and illustrated it on the same page. "The calabar bean."

Fascinated by the belladonna, Maya reached out to touch one of its berries.

"Don't!" cried Joe. "They're deadly!"

Maya jerked her hand away. In doing so, her arm brushed a leaf of the plant growing next to it. She gave a yelp of pain.

"What is it?" hissed Joe.

"That leaf *stung*!" She clutched her arm and frowned at the innocent-looking foliage, muttering: "I'm beginning not to like this garden."

"Hmmmm," said Joe. "That looks like poison sumac. In a minute, you'll come out in a rash."

Sure enough, an angry red mark soon appeared on Maya's arm.

"This still doesn't get us any closer to proving that Ankhe's the culprit," she said grumpily. "Anyone could have come here and picked the belladonna berries."

A rustling sound in the nearby darkness made both of them freeze.

"What was that?" wheezed Joe.

Maya pointed a shaking finger at something in the undergrowth.

Joe almost fell back in shock at the sight of a pair of glowing green eyes staring at them from a bush.

Then it made a noise. It sounded like… purring.

"It's a cat!" Maya almost laughed.

Joe breathed again – and a thought occurred to him. "Quick! Let's catch it. It might be Bes, Queen Ankhe's missing pet!"

He plunged after it, closely followed by Maya. They tore through the thick vegetation, as the cat turned tail and fled. Minutes later, they reached the garden's outer wall. The cat was nowhere to be seen. They leaned against the mud-brick wall and caught their breath. "We could have bought Ankhe's trust with that cat," said Joe despondently. "We could have questioned her, maybe found out if she really is the guilty one."

Footsteps approached along the path.

"Guards!" whispered Maya, and she pulled Joe deeper into the shadow of the wall.

Joe could make out the figures of two burly men moving towards them. The woody stem of a creeper was digging uncomfortably into his back. He shifted to get more comfortable and his hand brushed against a large, fleshy seed pod dangling from a branch of the creeper. Joe glanced down at it, and his mouth dropped open in astonishment. The pod was a long brown oval with a rough surface and a pointy tip. It was *exactly* like the illustration in that medieval book. The creeper, he noted, had large, pale pink flowers. There could be no doubt: this was the calabar bean – the antidote to belladonna poisoning!

Joe quickly broke off the pod from its branch. Unfortunately, this made a loud snapping sound just as the guards were passing. They lurched to a halt and, lifting their lanterns, peered into the darkness where Joe and Maya were huddled. Before the children could even think about escaping, the guards charged up and seized them, hauling them both to their feet.

Joe quickly shoved the seed pod in his pocket as he was manhandled onto the path. Then the two of them were marched at spear point out of the garden and into the king's apartment. They were taken straight to Lord Ay, who was at that moment in the royal bedchamber, standing vigil over the sickly king. Also there at Tut's bedside were Ay's wife, Tey, and the royal physician. There was no sign of Queen Ankhe.

The king was groaning feebly, muttering things that made no sense, as the physician cooled his brow with a damp cloth.

"We've found the escaped prisoner and her friend," the guard reported to Lord Ay.

"Good work," said Ay. He peered more closely at Joe. "Yes, I recall you from this morning. You helped rescue the thief, Bek, from the jaws of that crocodile – tried to defy the will of the gods." He glanced at the delirious Tut. "The king and I disagreed on the matter of whether to trust you, but I see now that I was right all along. You are nothing but a pair of rogues. Guards, take them to the royal dungeon. They will be executed at dawn, together with their friend Bek."

"Wait!" cried Joe desperately, as the guards began dragging them towards the door. "I have a cure for the king's illness!"

"What?" shouted the physician.

"Halt! Bring them back!" said Ay to the guards, and Joe and Maya were hauled before him once more.

"What nonsense is this?" frowned Ay.

"I believe the king has been poisoned," explained Joe.

"Really?" questioned Ay.

"That's ridiculous," scoffed Tey. "Who on earth would want to poison our beloved pharaoh?"

"I'm not sure who," admitted Joe, "but I *do* know that this is the antidote." He pulled the seed pod from his pocket. "This is from the calabar bean. I found it in the royal garden."

Ay took the pod from Joe and examined it suspiciously. "How do you know?"

"I–I have studied poisons, and how to cure them," stammered Joe.

Tey laughed scornfully at this, revealing her missing front tooth. "Why should we believe you, boy? For all we know, you yourself could be the poisoner, come to finish off your work."

"I promise you, I'm telling the truth!" cried Joe. "This will save the king."

"What do you think, doctor?" asked Ay, handing him the pod.

The physician squeezed the pod until it cracked, and three black seeds spilled into his palm. After examining them, he declared: "I have never heard or read of such seeds being used in any medicine. I think the boy is simply trying to save his own skin."

"I'm inclined to agree," said Ay. "Guards, take them away!"

Joe felt a chill of despair as the guard's rough hand clamped onto his shoulder.

"Wait," came a frail, croaking voice from the bed. "I want… I want you to try this, doctor."

Everyone stopped. The king must have emerged from his feverish state, because his request could not have been clearer.

"Joe is a good boy," croaked Tut. "I trust him…. Give me… his medicine."

"But Lord of the Universe…" objected Ay.

"I'm dying anyway," the king rasped. "Nothing has worked so far. We might as well…. We have nothing to lose…."

Ay looked furious. And, strangely, so did Tey. But the physician could not refuse a direct order from his king. He handed the beans to a servant and gave orders to mash and then boil them into a potion for Tut to drink.

The servant left, accompanied by Tey, who explained to her husband: "I want to make sure he does it properly."

Ay was instructing the guards to take Joe and Maya to the dungeon when, once again, Tut interrupted: "Let them stay," he said. "And if the medicine works, and I survive… I will shower them with honours." In a sadder voice, he added: "And if I die… then I can't stop you doing as you please with them."

Suppressing his irritation, Ay nodded at the guards and they unhanded Joe and Maya.

A little later, the servant returned with the potion. Tey did not return with him. He reported to Ay that she was tired and had retired to their villa.

The doctor stirred the brew and began administering it to the king.

From his corner of the room, Joe kept watch on the pale, still figure in the bed. All he could do now was wait, and pray that he was right about the calabar bean. Their lives – as well as Tut's – depended on it.

A soft sound from near the doorway distracted him. He turned to see who had entered and caught a glimpse of a figure lurking there in the shadows. The figure was holding something. Joe could see it glinting in the candlelight – something sharp and metallic.

A knife!

Chapter 9

Execution Day

Joe peered into the shadows, trying to get a closer look at the person who was loitering there. Everyone else was gathered at the king's bedside. No one noticed the figure creeping closer towards them.

Joe saw now that the newcomer was wearing a fine linen shift and had long, dark, plaited hair decorated with gold beads. She was clearly a woman, and a high-ranking one.

She must be after the king! Joe thought to himself.

But he was wrong. The assassin suddenly turned to Lord Ay, then raised her knife as if about to stab him.

"Stop! Look out!" Joe cried.

Ay whirled around in time to face his attacker. At the same moment, Joe sprang at the woman and pushed her over. Her knife clattered to the stone floor, coming to rest by Ay's feet.

"What is the meaning of this?" bellowed Ay.

The woman writhed like an angry viper beneath Joe's grip, until she managed to push him away.

Then she rose to her feet and leapt at Ay, clamping her hands around his neck in an attempt to strangle him. She might even have killed the grand vizier had the guards not intervened just then and dragged her away.

Everyone in the room stared in astonishment at the woman, scarcely able to believe their eyes – for it was none other than Queen Ankhe.

"Cat stealer!" she spat at Ay as she struggled to free herself from the guards. "How dare you take my poor Bes and imprison her without food or water! Poor thing could have died! I'll have you killed for this, Lord Ay! Guards, arrest him!"

Ay looked calmly at the guards and gave them a small shake of the head, then returned his attention to Ankhe.

"My queen," he said with icy politeness, "I did not imprison your cat. You have mistaken me for someone else."

"Then why did I find her, hidden in a cage in your villa just moments ago?"

Ay gave a start of surprise. "In my villa? What were you doing there?"

"A slave said she'd heard meowing from the courtyard, so I went to investigate. I couldn't believe it when I found Bes there. I was just freeing her when Tey turned up. She looked about as shocked as me at the sight of the poor cat, and swore she had nothing to do with it. So that leaves you, Lord Ay."

"I say again, this was not my doing," said Ay. "What would I want with your *cat*?" He placed a hand on her arm and gently but firmly steered her towards the door. "You've had a shock my lady. I suggest you go and get some rest."

"You've not heard the last of this, Ay," she protested as the guards led her away. "When my husband is better, he will punish you!"

"*If* your husband gets better," Ay muttered under his breath. To the head guard, he said: "Make sure she doesn't leave her quarters."

* * *

The king slept on through the night. His breathing remained weak, yet steady. It was impossible to tell if Joe's medicine was working or not. Eventually, the dawn came. Peach-coloured light streamed in through the window of Tut's bedroom. Outside, the acacia trees of the royal garden were alive with birdsong.

"The time has come," said Ay. He ordered the guards to fetch the prisoner Bek from the dungeon and bring him to the steps of the Temple of Amun-Re on the banks of the Nile. Ay told the physician to send word of any change in the king's condition, then turned to address the others in the room: "All who wish to see the justice of the gods carried out, follow me."

As they left the apartment, Maya couldn't help noticing how beautiful the garden looked in the early morning light – yet even this failed to lift her spirits.

"We did all we could," said Joe in an attempt to cheer her up.

"Well, it wasn't enough," responded Maya, "and now an innocent person is about to die. We may as well go back to the 21st century. I'm not sure I want to see this."

"Let's just wait a little longer," Joe reassured his cousin. "You never know what might happen."

At length, they reached the Temple of Amun-Re. On a flat area between the bottom of the temple steps and the river stood Bek, surrounded by guards. His hands and feet had been securely bound with rope to which heavy stones had been attached to act as weights. Bek looked wretched – pale and hunched over. Maya could barely look as he was forced into a boat and rowed out towards the middle of the river.

She knew she had to do something to stop this – but what? They had no evidence that would persuade people of Bek's innocence.

Next to Maya stood General Horem and Tey, who had returned to observe the execution. Horem's face was solemn, but Tey seemed to be enjoying herself. Maya couldn't believe that the woman was actually smiling!

A chill breeze blew across the esplanade, ruffling tunics and kilts and making Maya shiver. She put her hands in her pockets for warmth and her left hand touched something soft and squishy. It was the fig she had found in Bek's apartment.

Taking it out, she scowled at it. *A fine piece of evidence you turned out to be!*

The teeth marks of whoever had bitten into it were clearly imprinted in its juicy flesh – Ankhe's teeth marks most likely, though Maya couldn't prove it. She was about to throw it away, when she noticed something. Peering closer, she saw that the teeth marks were very strange: there was a small chunk in the middle of the fig that should have been bitten but hadn't been. It was as if the biter had a tooth missing – a front tooth by the look of it.

Suddenly, Maya became extremely still. She tried to control her breathing as she glanced once more at Tey, just to be sure she hadn't made a mistake. Tey was still grinning – and Maya now knew she was right: Tey's front tooth was missing. So it was *Tey*, not Ankhe, who had planted the necklace at Bek's house!

Then Maya noticed something else: a livid red rash on Tey's forearm. It was just like the one Maya herself had received from the poison sumac growing next to the belladonna plant. Tey must have picked the berries to poison the king! Tey was behind everything!

But was it too late?

With a shudder, Maya saw that the oarsmen out on the river had stopped rowing. Two guards had raised Bek from his seat. As he wriggled and squirmed in their arms, they prepared to throw him to the now circling crocodiles.

"S-Stop!!" Maya spluttered at the top of her voice. "Don't push him in! He's innocent! I have proof!"

The guards turned in bewilderment towards the river bank. Joe, too, stared at Maya, wondering what she was playing at.

"What is the meaning of this?" Ay roared at her. "How dare you attempt, once again, to defy the will of the gods?" Then he called out to the guards in the boat: "Proceed with the execution!"

"Hold on!" interjected Horem. "If the girl has proof of this man's innocence, I for one would like to see it – preferably *before* we let him die!"

"I warn you not to get involved in my business, General," snarled Ay. "You have no authority over how criminals are dealt with in this kingdom!"

"Maybe not, but *I* have," came a fragile voice behind them.

Everyone turned in surprise to see King Tut standing at the top of the temple steps. He looked tired and weak as he leaned upon his staff – yet a healthy glow had returned to his cheeks. Joe's medicine must have worked!

"Lord of the Sun and Stars!" exclaimed the startled Ay. "A miracle!"

"Stop the execution," ordered Tut, "and let us listen to what the girl has to say."

Grudgingly, Ay told the oarsmen to bring the prisoner back to shore.

When he arrived there, Bek looked up at Maya in wide-eyed gratitude. In fact, all eyes were now upon Maya, as they waited impatiently for her to reveal her 'proof'.

Trying her best to stay calm, Maya said: "I know Bek didn't steal the necklace… because…" she pointed at Tey, "… because *she* did."

This accusation provoked outraged gasps from several people on the steps, but

Maya continued: "Tey took out the jewel, then placed the necklace in Bek's house so that he'd get the blame. And she used belladonna berries from the royal garden to try and kill the king."

Chapter 10

The Evidence

"Infamy!" shrieked Ay. "Treason!" His cheeks went purple with rage and flecks of spit flew out of his mouth as he bawled curses at Maya. Then he turned to the king and begged him to give permission for her immediate execution for daring to accuse his noble, virtuous wife of such unspeakable crimes.

"These are very serious charges," Tut said to Maya. "I hope for your sake you can back them up."

"I can, Lord of the Universe," said Maya, and she held up the fig. "I found this under Bek's bed yesterday. It was fresh when I found it, so it must have been dropped there the night before." She showed it to Tut. "See, it has a strange bite mark…. It was bitten by someone with a missing front tooth, like Tey."

Before Tut could respond, Tey strode up to Maya and plucked the fig from her fingers. She glanced at it, then threw back her head and laughed. "That's it?" she chortled. "That's all you've got? A fig? My dear girl, who can say *where* you found this? The city dump? Perhaps someone else in Thebes has a missing tooth and a liking for figs. It's hardly proof, is it?"

"I found it at Bek's home," insisted Maya.

"Did you now?" smirked Tey. "Well, let's imagine for a moment you're right – let's say I really did plant the necklace at Bek's house. How do you suppose I obtained the necklace in the first place? Hm? Did I turn into mist and pass magically through the golden door of the royal treasury?"

Maya didn't know what to say. She hadn't even thought about how Tey had got hold of the necklace.

At that moment, Joe blinked in surprise. His eyebrows shot up as something very significant occurred to him. "You stole the key to the treasury from General Horem," he said to Tey. "I saw you slip it back into his pocket yesterday afternoon."

For the first time, Tey seemed to lose some of her composure. "This is ridiculous!" she snapped.

"Wait…." frowned Horem, feeling for something in his pocket. "The young man may be on to something." He pulled out the golden key. "I lost this several days ago… come to think of it, that was after a visit to your villa, Tey. And then last night it miraculously reappeared – again after a visit to your villa. You took the key in order to steal the necklace!"

Tey laughed once more, though with less confidence. "These are absurd fabrications," she tittered, "based on absolutely no evidence." Then she turned on Maya. "And does your fig prove that I poisoned the king, too?"

"No," said Maya, "but *that* does." She pointed to the rash on Tey's arm.

"It's a rash from poison sumac," said Joe, "which we found growing next to the belladonna in the royal garden. You must have got that when you picked the poisonous berries."

Tey self-consciously covered the rash with her hand. She began to tremble. "Why do you just stand there, husband?"

she said to Ay. "Come to my aid. Tell these wicked people that they are liars and will be punished for the terrible things they're saying."

Ay put a protective arm around Tey. "Do not worry, dear. First we shall prove you innocent, and then we shall deal with them."

"I think a search of Ay and Tey's villa might be a good way to start the investigation," suggested Horem. The general looked immensely pleased with the way events were developing. With the king well again, and his chief rival's wife in deep trouble, life could hardly be sweeter.

Tut agreed to the plan, despite Ay's protests, and the royal party returned to the grand vizier's villa.

* * *

The guards went to work searching the interior of the villa, while Joe and Maya checked the courtyard. In one corner was the kitchen with its clay oven.

While they were searching the area for clues, the king appeared. For once, he was without his escort of guards and servants.

"Hello, my friends," he smiled. "I wanted to thank you… for finding that medicine. I'm feeling a great deal better."

Bowing, Joe said: "I'm so pleased, my lord."

Tut made his way over to the oven. On top of it sat a dish of small cakes. The king leaned down and sniffed them. "Ah, my favourites," he breathed. "Date and honey cakes. Tey makes the best ones, you know. She bakes them for me personally."

Joe and Maya swapped glances. "Does she, my lord?" asked Maya.

"Oh yes. Her servant often brings them to me."

"And how long has this been going on for," asked Joe.

"Oh, several moons now," said Tut. "I think I might try one now, in fact…."

"No!" cried Joe and Maya together.

Joe broke open one of the cakes and took out something – a small black berry. He showed it to Tut.

"What is that? Some sort of herb?"

"Belladonna, sire," answered Joe. "The poison that was killing you!"

Tut's jaw dropped open.

"So it *was* Tey! I never believed it possible… until now!"

They went back inside the villa. Ay and Tey were standing in the middle of the hall, looking angry and defiant, as guards searched their possessions. Joe showed

Ay the charred berry. "Tey was putting belladonna into the cakes she gave to the king," he said.

"Never!" gasped Ay, as Tey burst into tears.

"She couldn't have known these berries were poisonous!" Ay shook his wife. "Tell me Tey! Tell me you didn't know!"

Just then, Horem uttered a triumphant cheer. He was standing by the chest – the same chest Joe had hidden in. In the palm of his hand nestled a beautiful yellow gemstone. "I found it in here," he said, "under all the linen."

"My jewel!" whooped Tut. "My precious jewel!" He hobbled over and took it from Horem.

Seeing this, Ay let go of his wife, who collapsed to the floor where she continued sobbing. Ay looked at her with disdain. "Why, Tey?" he asked.

"I wanted y-you to become pharaoh, husband," she wept. "I knew if we had the jewel, the g-gods would favour you."

Tey wiped her eyes and tried to regain her composure. "I tried to pin the blame for the theft on Ankhe and Bek. After I stole the necklace and removed the gem, I disguised myself as Ankhe, painting a mole on my cheek, then went to Bek's house where I planted the necklace. I even stole the queen's cat, hoping she would blame its disappearance on the king, giving her a motive to kill him.

"It would have worked, too – except that I could never resist a fig, and Bek had a bowl of them on the table in his house. I heard a noise outside and must have dropped it in fright. That was my biggest mistake."

"The mystery is solved and all is well again," said Tut, cradling his treasured gem.

"An innocent man is saved, and I have my jewel back. And it's mainly thanks to the valiant efforts of you, Joe and Maya."

He turned to them… but they were nowhere to be seen.

* * *

Once the jewel had been found, Joe and Maya had sneaked away. Their job was done, and their ancient Egyptian adventure was over.

Soon, they were at the quayside beyond the city wall, where Maya persuaded a kindly fisherman to take them back across the river. From there, it was a short hike to the Valley of the Kings, where they had made their original time jump.

Joe set the date on his phone, they held hands, and in a whirl of sparkling dust they were whisked back to the present day.

When they reappeared, they saw in front of them the door that led to the underground auditorium where the historians had gathered to hear about Tut's letter. They were about to make their way towards it when the door swung open and out stepped Professor Salma Boutros.

"Ah, there you are!" she called to them. "I was surprised to see you leave my lecture early. Where did you go to?"

"We… er… needed some fresh air," said Maya. "It was all so exciting!"

With a smile, Salma began walking towards a small car park. Joe and Maya ran after her.

"Tell me, professor," said Joe, "how long did Tutankhamun reign?"

Salma stopped and turned to him in surprise. "I'd have thought you'd have known the answer to that. We believe he reigned for thirty long and happy years."

Joe glanced at Maya, and she smiled at him. So they *had* changed history. Tut hadn't died young, after all.

"But the letter," persisted Joe. "What about the letter he wrote in the ninth year of his reign saying he was dying?"

"Yes, that's a puzzle," admitted Salma. "I suppose the king must have survived his illness.... Most fortunate. But it's great to have the letter, isn't it? Written by King Tut himself."

"Or by his scribe," suggested Joe.

Salma nodded. "Yes, indeed. I'm sure that scribe could not imagine how famous his words would one day turn out to be!"

THE END

FICTI●N EXPRESS

THE READERS TAKE CONTROL!

Have you ever wanted to change the course of a plot, change a character's destiny, tell an author what to write next?

Well, now you can!

'The Tale of Tutankhamun's Treasure' was originally written for the award-winning interactive e-book website Fiction Express.

Fiction Express e-books are published in gripping weekly episodes. At the end of each episode, readers are given voting options to decide where the plot goes next. They vote online and the winning vote is then conveyed to the author who writes the next episode, in real time, according to the readers' most popular choice.

www.fictionexpress.co.uk

WINNER
Education Resources
Award for Innovation

FICTION EXPRESS

TALK TO THE AUTHORS

The Fiction Express website features a blog where readers can interact with the authors while they are writing. An exciting and unique opportunity!

FANTASTIC TEACHER RESOURCES

Each weekly Fiction Express episode comes with a PDF of teacher resources packed with ideas to extend the text.

"The teaching resources are fab and easily fill a whole week of literacy lessons!"
Rachel Humphries, teacher at Westacre Middle School

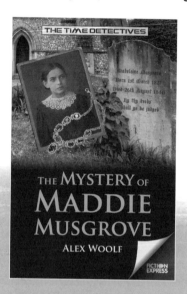

FICTI🌑N EXPRESS

The Time Detectives:
The Disappearance of Danny Doyle
by Alex Woolf

In this latest adventure in the Time Detectives series, Joe and Maya are exploring a ruined castle in Scotland when they uncover the story of a stolen chalice and a curse that led to the castle's downfall 750 years ago. Journeying back to the 13th century, they embark on a search for the chalice, hoping to restore the castle's fortunes. Will they succeed or will the castle fall 'to wrack and ruin' as the curse foretold?

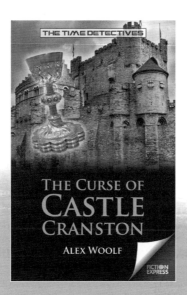

ISBN 978-1-78322-581-1

The Golden Amulet
An Anglo-Saxon Adventure
by Alex Woolf

Gisela, the daughter of an Anglo-Saxon chieftain, is a brave and skilful archer. When her village is attacked by a band of fierce Vikings and her parents are kidnapped, Gisela has a decision to make. Can she trust her uncle, Oswald, who is now in charge of the village? Or is he too friendly with the Vikings?

Should Gisela risk everything and try to rescue her parents? And who can she trust on her perilous quest?

ISBN 978-1-78322-597-2

FICTI🗩N EXPRESS

Threads
by Sharon Gosling

Young Charlie Thwaite works in Stanton's mill and is best friends with the mill-owner's daughter, Clara. When Charlie's father is wrongly accused of sabotaging Stanton's new spinning machines, it's up to Charlie and Clara to prove his innocence.

Will they discover the real culprit in time to save both Charlie's father and the mill?

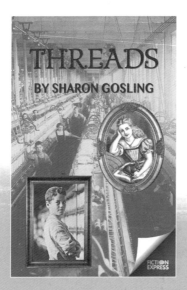

ISBN 978-1-78322-557-6

About the Author

Alex Woolf was born in London in 1964. He played drums in a teen band and, in his 20s, he rode his motorbike and travelled in America (where he nearly ended up as a barracuda's lunch!). In between, he also did lots of dull and dangerous jobs. His worst job was washing up in a restaurant kitchen full of cockroaches!

Finally, he settled down to write books. Alex has written non-fiction books on subjects like sharks, robots and the Black Death, but his greatest love is writing fiction, and he claims to have been writing stories almost since he was able to hold a pen.

His books for Fiction Express include other titles in his Time Detectives series, *Mind Swap*, a story in which a bully and his victim change places, and *The Golden Amulet*, an Anglo-Saxon adventure. He has also written *Chronosphere*, a science-fiction trilogy about a world in which time moves super-slow, and *Aldo Moon and the Ghost of Gravewood Hall*, a story about a teenage Victorian detective who investigates ghosts in a spooky old mansion.